# Goodbye, Berry

By Chaya Shinhav
Illustrated by Mike Eagle

A HIPPY Storybook

Connelly-3-Publishing Group, Inc.
Guilford, CT 06437

This book is available in the United States in both English and Spanish editions. Original English translation from Hebrew by David Kriss. English edition edited by Nina Harel and Gail M. Griffin. Spanish translation services provided by C. C. Writer. Spanish edition edited by Lisa Clyde Nielsen.

10   9

Published in the United States by Connelly-3-Publishing Group, Inc.
Guilford, CT 06437

Berry wanted to go away. He wanted to go to a different place, a better place, and a more beautiful place.

He said goodbye to his bed, closed the door with the picture of a strawberry on it, and left.

Goodbye, Berry!

Berry walked and walked until he came to a big field.

In the field there were three trees: one very tall tree, one not-so-tall tree, and one small tree. And on the small tree perched a bird.

"Chirp, chirp! Where are you going?" asked the bird.

"I'm going to a different place, a better place, and a more beautiful place," said Berry.

"I want to come too," said the bird.

So the bird said goodbye to the three trees and flew off with Berry.

Goodbye, bird!

Berry and the bird continued on their way. They went farther and farther until they came to a little hill. The hill was completely covered in green grass. And on top of the hill stood a goat eating grass.

"Maaa, maaa. Where are you going?" asked the goat.

"We are going to a different place, a better place, and a more beautiful place," said Berry.

"I want to come too," said the goat.

So he said goodbye to the little hill and set off with the others.

Goodbye, goat!

They went farther and farther until they reached the sea. And on the sea was a ship. And on the ship there were many sailors.

"Hello there!" called the sailors. "Where are you going?"

"We're going to a different place, a better place, and a more beautiful place," said Berry. "Perhaps you know of such a place?"

"No!" the sailors called back. "We have sailed to many places all over the world, but we have never seen such a place!"

Then smoke blew out of the stack, and the ship sailed off into the distance.

Goodbye, ship!

Berry, the bird, and the goat went farther and farther, until suddenly they spotted a small airplane flying in the sky. The airplane flew toward them.

The pilot looked through the window and called out, "Hello there! Where are you going?"

"We're going to a different place, a better place, and a more beautiful place," said Berry. "Perhaps you know of such a place?"

"No!" the pilot called back. "I have flown over many places in the world, but I have never seen such a place!"

Then the airplane flew away and disappeared into the blue skies.

Goodbye, airplane.

Berry, the bird, and the goat went farther and farther until they came to a very wide road. And on the road there were many cars. They were all going to the big city.

"Perhaps that is the place we are looking for," cried Berry.

And so they too hurried off to the big city. They arrived in the city. The buildings were very, very tall. The streets were very, very long. There were lots of shops and there were many people.

Berry, the bird, and the goat wandered around the big city. The honking of the cars frightened them. A boy carrying lots of packages bumped into them.

They wandered and wandered until they were tired out. Their feet hurt them, and they had no strength left.

The goat was hungry. He saw grass in a little garden and wanted to eat it. But a man came out of the house and drove him away.

The bird was tired. She looked for a place to rest and perched on top of a chimney. But black smoke came out of the chimney. It made her feathers dirty, and she couldn't see a thing.

Berry was tired and hungry, too. But he did not know the people in the city, and there was no house there for him to go to.

"Maaa, maaa," said the goat. "I've walked far enough and have seen enough things today. Now I want to go back to *my* hill."

"Chirp, chirp," said the bird. "I have flown far enough and have seen enough things today. Now I want to go back to *my* three trees."

"And I have walked far enough and have seen enough things today as well," said Berry. "Fields, mountains, the sea, and even a ship and an airplane and the big city. But now I want to go back to *my* house."

And so they turned around and started on their way back.

The goat saw his little hill from far away, and it looked so beautiful! It was the most beautiful hill he had ever seen.

The goat was very happy and quickly ran off to the hill. And he lives there still.

Goodbye, goat!

The bird saw her three trees from far away, and they looked so beautiful! They were the most beautiful trees she had ever seen.

The bird was very happy and quickly flew off to her trees. And she lives there still.

Goodbye, bird!

Berry saw his little house from far away, and the house looked so good and beautiful! It was the best and most beautiful house he had ever seen.

Berry was very happy and quickly ran to the house.

He opened the door with the picture of a strawberry on it and walked inside.

Goodbye, Berry!